The Bird and The Hippo

written by Becky Pierce (age 10)
pictures by Karin Exter

Bywater Press
Bellingham, Washington

Published by Bywater Press, Bellingham, Washington
www.bywaterpress.com

First edition, first printing
ISBN: 978-1-7330675-2-2

B C D E F G H I K

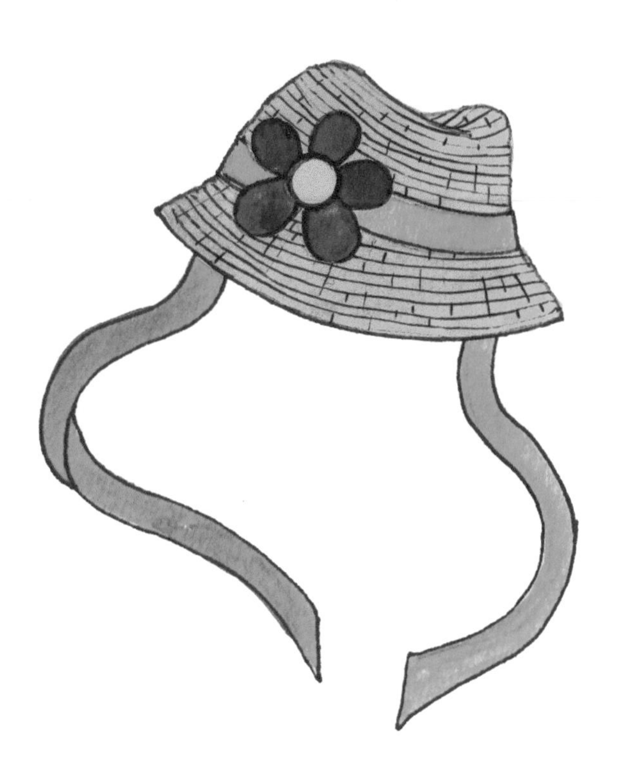

Well, it all started in a big river in Kenya, Africa. It was somewhere around spring and all the birds were coming back. It just so happened that one of the birds wasn't watching where it was going and it crashed into a tree. Down, down, down he went till he hit something hard.

But he didn't hit the water. He didn't hit a rock. Although it did look much like a rock. It was a dark gray color. It was a hippo. It was a lady hippo!

Lady hippo looked back and said, "Oh, no, not another one! Every year the same thing! A male bird is all excited and hits something. It seems like I'm the target for birds!"

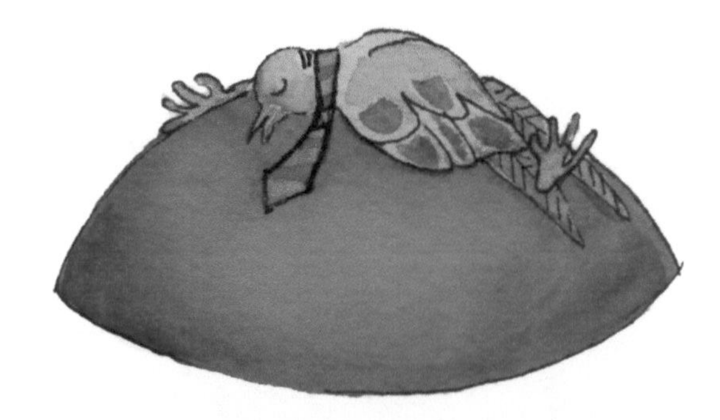

The bird woke up. He said, "Where am I?"

"You're on my back. Can't you see?" said the hippo.

The bird looked up. "But where am I? I mean what city? What town? I hope it's Hollywood, California! I want to get into the movies."

"Hollywood, California?" exclaimed the hippo. "Why, that's half way around the world from here! This is Africa."

"Africa!?" exclaimed the bird, filled with shame. "I knew I should have made that left turn in Germany. Oh well, I might as well make the best of it."

"Yes," said the hippo. "Well, you're probably hungry, so come on and I'll show you where the food is."

So the bird ate and a few months went by. It was late summer and the bird and the hippo were resting.

"Hey," said the bird, "what is your name anyway?" The hippo looked puzzled. "Well, let me put it another way. What do animals call you?"

"Oh that," said the hippo. "Everyone calls me Middy."

"My name is Fritz," said the bird.

The hippo started laughing. "Fritz? That's a funny name for a bird. Ha, ha!"

"Well!" said the bird. "Middy's a funny name for a hippo. You're not very middy to me."

"Well," said the hippo, now very red in her face and turning redder, "you can just get off my back!"

"That suits me just fine." The bird flew to shore and said, "I didn't like your back anyway! It's lumpy!"

The hippo started crying. Before nightfall they made up and were friends again.

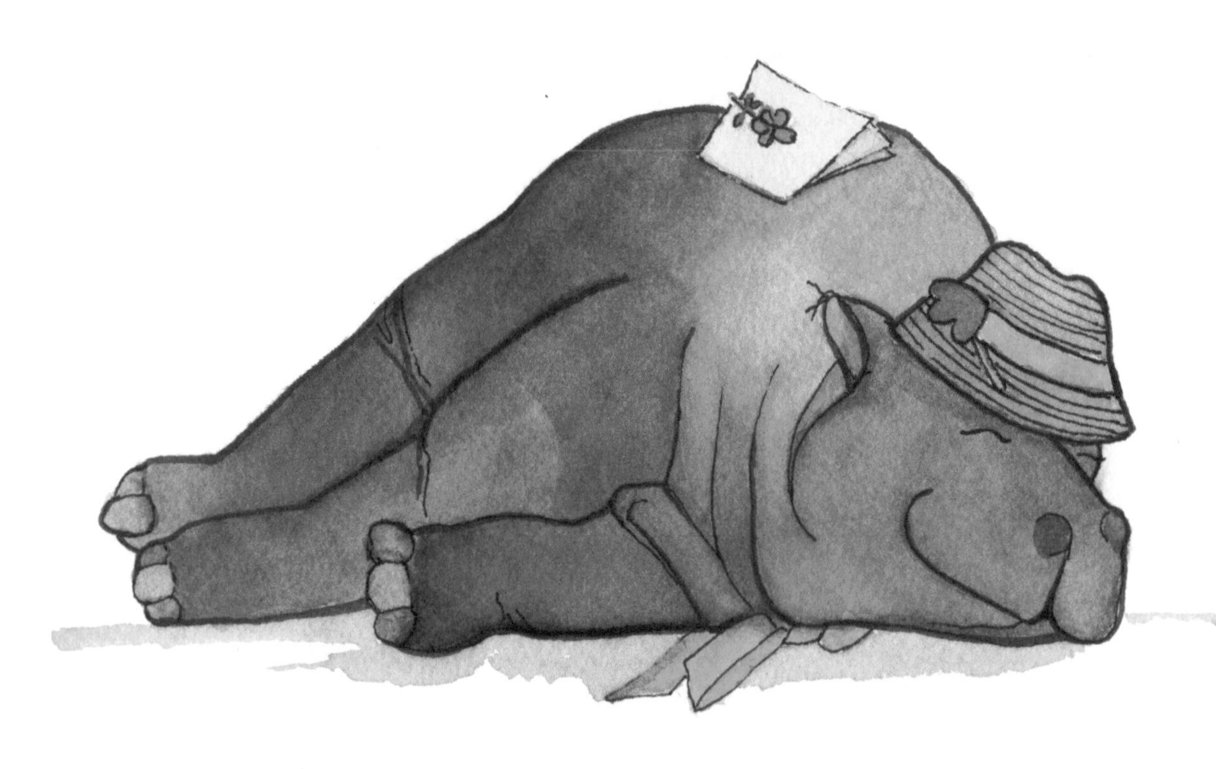

It was getting colder by the day and one
morning the hippo woke up. She looked
on her back and found a note. It said,

Good-bye Middy. I'm sorry
but I had to migrate last
night. I didn't want to wake
you up, and my flock was
flying above me.

Yours truly
Fritz

But the time passed quickly. It was near spring.

Then suddenly, *CRASH!* Fritz came crashing down right on Middy.

"Fritz, oh, Fritz! I missed you so much," said Middy.

"You haven't changed a bit," said Fritz.

Then all of a sudden they heard a voice calling, "Fritz, Fritz, where are you?"

"Here I am!" said Fritz, calling back. They saw a beautiful bird come gliding down and sit on the hippo.

The bird said, "Oh, who's your friend?"

Middy glanced at Fritz, "Well, who is she? Just don't stand there! Introduce us."

Fritz introduced them and they all became very good friends. Fritz told Middy that the bird's name was Heidi and they were married.

Heidi was going to have some little chicks and she built a nest on Middy's back.

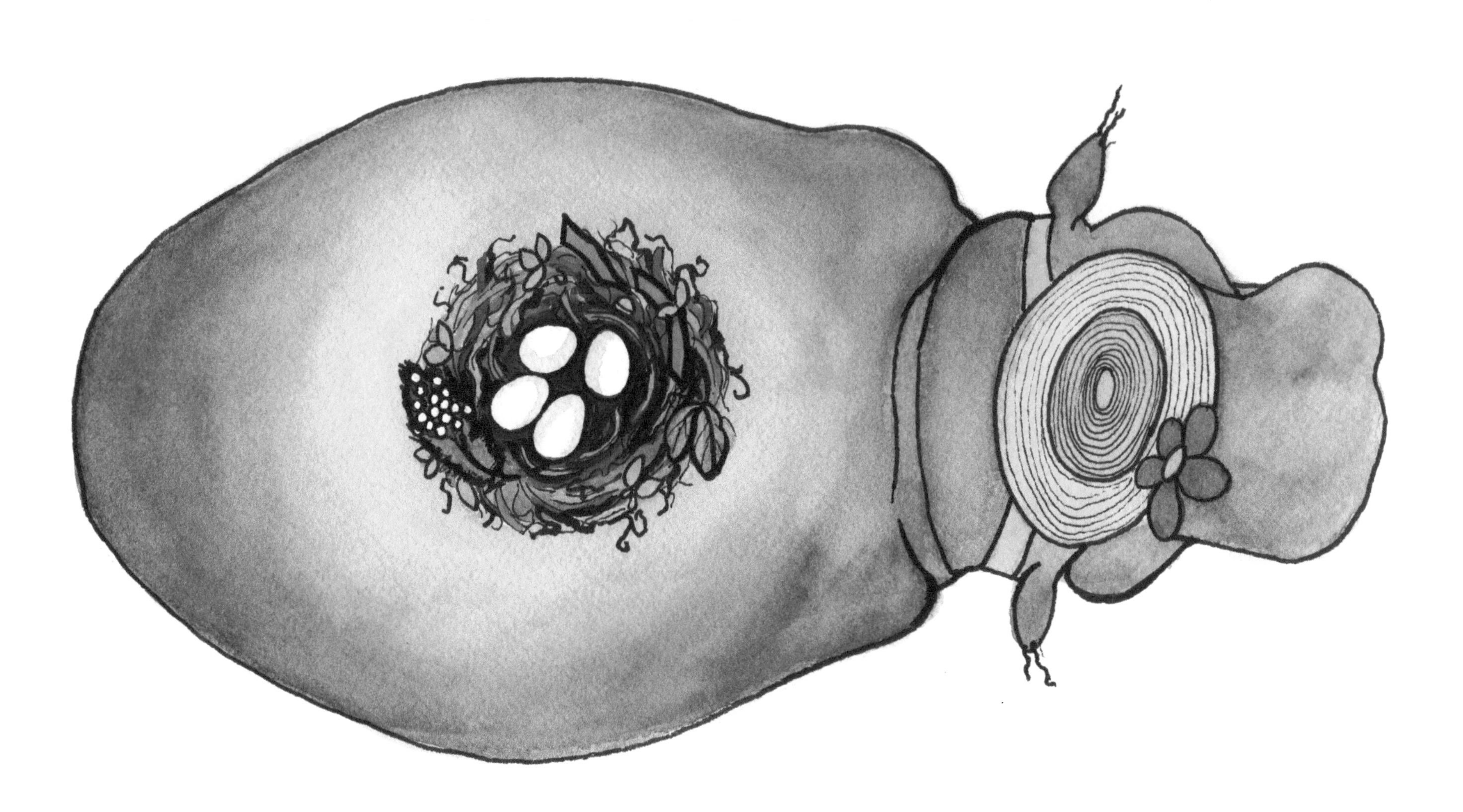

One cool evening, Heidi woke up. She shook Fritz, "Fritz, Fritz, wake up!" Fritz woke up.

"Why did you wake me up?" he sputtered.

"The eggs are hatching!"

Just then Middy woke up. "What's all the excitement?" she said in a mad voice.

"My eggs are hatching."

Just then all four eggs hatched. There were two girls and two boys. They were all very healthy.

It was getting near winter and all the birds learned to fly.

One day, Fritz heard a sound up in the sky. He looked up and he saw his flock flying above him.

He gathered everyone together and they started packing. When they'd gotten everything packed they waved good-bye to Middy and set off on their long flight to Germany.

Forever
friends

They visited Middy every chance they got and always brought her presents.

So if it wasn't for that wrong right turn in
Germany, they wouldn't have met Middy.

The End

Becky, This is grea[t]
maybe we could put it
in the book,
if you'd ...? Jan 28, 72

The bird and the Hippo

Passport photo, June 1971

Rebecca Pierce Murray discovered the Bird and Hippo story nearly 50 years after writing it while riffling through some old papers. Instantly, she knew she had found a treasure. She wrote the story in 1972 after her mother took Rebecca, her sister and two brothers, ages 7 to 11, on a trip to East Africa. They visited national wildlife preserves in Kenya and Tanzania where they actually watched hippos in the wild.

Upon their return, Rebecca entered the 5th grade where she met Mr. Kaiser, a teacher who emphasized storytelling and creative writing with his students. *The Bird and The Hippo* was one of many stories a young Rebecca would write and illustrate.

The story is a metaphor for life. Rebecca is Fritz, the bird who wants to make it big in Hollywood, but never does. Instead, Fritz makes a wrong turn and winds up In Africa. There, his life takes a new direction when he befriends a Lady Hippo named Middy. Together they learn the value of friendship, forgiveness, and silver linings.

Today, Rebecca, husband Steve, and their two dogs live on a 20-acre wildlife habitat in the beautiful Skagit Valley in Washington state. She satisfies her desire for stage and screen through a highly entertaining professional speaking style that she delivers to audiences around the world. Rebecca is a gifted storyteller who also showcases her talents behind the camera and in the studio as a photographer, videographer and presentation coach. In bringing *The Bird and The Hippo* back to life, Rebecca hopes to remind others that childhood aspirations can remain a source of inspiration for creative adventures later in life.

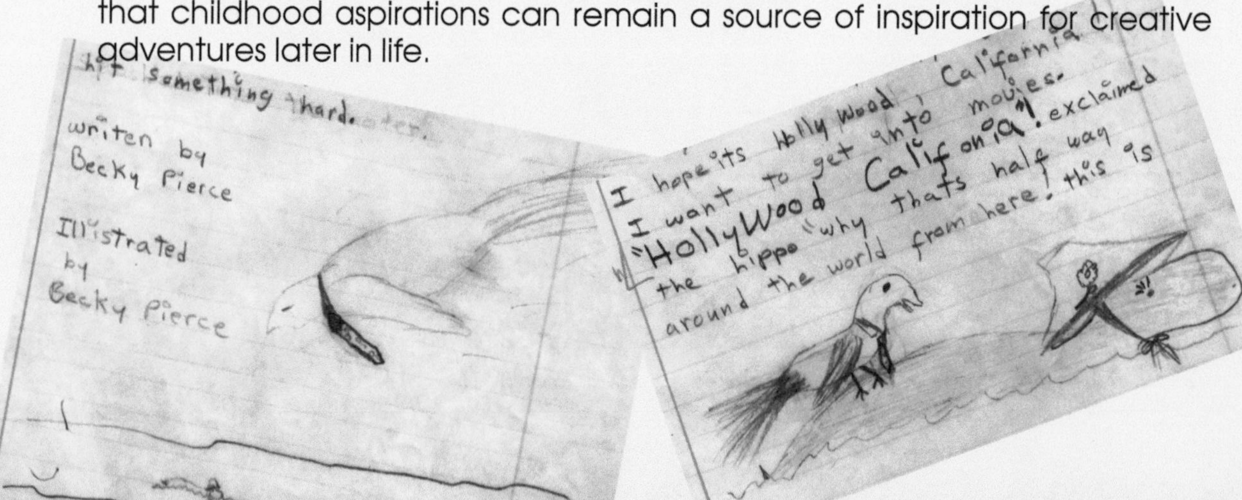
hit something hard.

writen by
Becky Pierce

Illistrated
by
Becky Pierce

I hope its Hollywood, California
I want to get into movies.
"Hollywood California"! exclaimed
the hippo "why thats half way
around the world from here! this is

Christmas Party, circa 1966

Karin Exter was born in South Africa with an insatiable thirst for visual beauty. From an early age she attended advanced art classes. When on vacation in the country's amazing national parks, Karin would often see hippos, antelopes, lions, hyenas and other wild animals roaming freely in the wild.

As a teen, Karin attended a prestigious fine arts school, winning numerous awards for her talents. She pursued a variety of careers including restaurateur and flight attendant, then, upon becoming a single parent, put her art on hold to raise her daughter.

It wasn't until 2002, nearly 20 years after she put down her paintbrush, that Karin returned to art with a renewed passion. Today when Karin is not kayaking, volunteer seal sitting or gardening, she spends much of her time in her Edmonds, Washington studio painting with oils.

Upon hearing Rebecca perform *The Bird and The Hippo* book at a social gathering, Karin fell in love with the story and was delighted with the opportunity to illustrate it. *The Bird and The Hippo* is Karin's first watercolor project and her first children's book.

Karin's strives to see the world as child would, by appreciating the beauty of things as they are.

CPSIA information can be obtained
at www.ICGtesting.com
Printed in the USA
BVHW061508140221
599955BV00001BA/2